# SCOOBY-DOO! PICTURE CLUE BOOK

# THE CHRISTMAS COOKIE CASE

### By Maria S. Barbo
### Illustrated by Duendes del Sur

## Hello Reader — Level 1

Visit Scholastic.com for information about our books and authors online!

ISBN 0-439-55714-3

14 13 12 11

11 12 13 14 15/0

Designed by Maria Stasavage
Printed in the U.S.A.   40
First printing, November 2003

P9-BBV-001

## SCHOLASTIC INC.
New York  Toronto  London  Auckland  Sydney
Mexico City  New Delhi  Hong Kong  Buenos Aires

It was the week before Christmas.

Christmas Eve was coming fast.
 and his friends were at the
 .

They had to help get ready!

and helped bake

.

put and small on

his .

put in his .

made a giant .

They could not wait to taste the

!

But the  were too hot to eat.

 put the  by the  to

cool.

Then  went to help the elves

make .

 and  were hungry.

What could they eat?

They ate  ,  ,  , and

 !

Then  saw 's .

He put on the .

"Look, ," said . "I'm !

Ho, ho, ho!" said .

put on 's and .

"I'm !" said . "Ro! Ro! Ro!"

and laughed.

Their bellies shook like bowls full

of jelly.

"That was fun, !"  said.

"But now I need some ."

 and  looked at the .

The  were gone!

"Ruh-roh!" said .

"Maybe a  took the ," said .

"Run!" said .

"Hide!" said .

and  ran outside.

 ran into  .

 hid in the snow.

 was putting lights on the

 .

Did  eat the  ?

"  !  !" said  and  .

"We have to find the  !"

 and  found  .

 was making  .

 put a  on a  .

Did  take the cookies?

"! !" said  and .

"We have to find the !"

 and  looked for .

 was singing with Mrs. Claus.

"Jingle ! Jingle !"

Did  hide the ?

and  did not know what

to do.

, , and  did not eat the

.

Maybe a  *did* take the !

 and  were scared.

"Run!" said .

"Hide!" said .

ran into 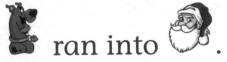.

 hid under the Christmas

.

 looked at 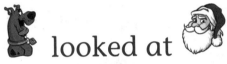.

 has a big belly.

Did  eat the ?

 found 🎁 under the 🎄.

And the 🎁 were filled with 🔔!

🎅 did not eat the 🔔.

A 👹 did not take the 🔔.

The 🔔 were Christmas 🎁!

"Merry Christmas to all," said 🎅.

"And for all some good 🔔!"

Did you spot all the picture clues in this Scooby-Doo mystery?

Each picture clue is on a flash card. Ask a grown-up to cut out the flash cards. Then try reading the words on the back of the cards. The pictures will be your clue.

Reading is fun with Scooby-Doo!

| | |
|---|---|
| Shaggy | Scooby |
| Fred | Velma |
| Santa | Daphne |

| cookies | North Pole |
| gumdrops | Scooby Snacks |
| window | gingerbread Velma |

| turkey | toys |
| :---: | :---: |
| coat | candy canes |
| boots | hat |

tree

snow monster

truck

wheel

gifts

bells